Hear Me Out

Jonessi

Hear Me Out

Jonessi

DEDICATION

Me, Myself and I are loving ourselves, the thoughts we come up with
and the conversations we have

ACKNOWLEDGEMENTS

I want to thank the creativity of things I experienced and everything in life that has happen to me and helped in this process

Table of Contents

You ever played cards

You never know what you're dealt

Have you tried gambling with those unknown cards?

It is hard, isn't it!

Sometimes you win

Sometimes you lose

You learn and do it again

Sometimes you gain money, little power and feeling of being alive

Sometimes you lose everything and have to seek help

Don't get to overly excited

Just enjoy all what the cards thrown at you

Are you ready to play?

Isolation

Fear

Decisions

I want to enjoy the good

Old days and the days ahead

Do you know how to handle the problem ahead?

You winging it but oblivious to your own stupidity

Fear

Isolation

Decisions

Wake up

Wake up

What is with you?

Explore and except

What is with you?

Understanding who you dealing with

What is with you?

You bitchy for no reason

What is with you?

You always want something in return

What is with you?

Didn't I take care and help you

What is with you?

Do you even appreciate anything?

What is with you?

Your being a pain to deal

What is with you?

I'm tired of trying

What is with you?

You don't understand or try to

What is with you?

What is with you?

Memories

Playing

No Worries

Fun

Sadness

Anger

Deception

Trust

No Trust

Love

No Love

Taking

Wanting

Caregiver

Being Cared For

Friends

Troubles

Honesty

Learning

Growing

More memories to come and go

Will it Fade or Stay

Will you have someone to reminisce with

Will photos help you remember

Memories

Listen

Damn

Pain

Aggravated

Listen

Damn

Nerve Racking

Listen

Understand

Damn

Listen

See

Listen

Listen!

Galaxy

Stars

Light Years

Aliens

Beings

Universe

Beyond

Unknown

Planets

Above

Unreachable

Detained

Unintentional

Why did you leave like that?

Did phone really ring?

Was you embarrassed?

It happens; shit happens

No text or call

Was your ego hurt?

Why you decided not to come back?

It happens; shit happens

Was it a blow to all your egos?

It messed things up

I was a little upset

Not what you're thinking

It happens; shit happens

Occurrences' get in the way

Why are you silent?

You're hurt and embarrassed

It happens; shit happens

He loves me

He loves me not

He loves my happiness

He love my kindness

He love my strongness

He loves me not

He loves me not my craziness

He loves me not my attitude

He loves me not my flaws

He loves me

He loves me not

He loves me no matter what

Take Me

Take me there

Take me here

Take me everywhere

Take me to bliss

Take me to nirvana

Take me to moon and stars

Take me to heavens and earth

Take me there

Take me here

Take me everywhere

Pain

Pain I see

Pain I hear

Will the pain stop

Will the pain go away

Will I see if subdued

Will I see if it loses luster

Will the crying evaporate

Will the bruises go away

Will it leave an everlasting mark

Will you understand the pain I'm in

Will you help me heal

Will you evaluate the pain

Pain

Pain I see

Pain I hear

$ Money $

What will you do for the dollar?

What will you do for the dinero?

What will you do for the yen?

What will you do for the pound?

Does the money make you jump for joy?

Does the money give you happiness?

Will you sell your soul for the money?

Did the dinero give you everlasting joy?

Did the pound solve all the problems?

What will you do for the $$$$$$$?

PEN

Pen is very mighty

Pen + Voice even more mighty

Pen + Voice + Ears is inspiring mightiness

Pen + Voice + Ears + Understanding is inspiring mightiness changes

Pen is always mightier than the sword

But Pen with sharp sword does come in handy

Blood

Blood Rising

Blood Pumping

Blood Boiling

Blood Blue

Blood Red

Blood Overflowing

Blood Clouts

Blood Infectious

Blood Veins

Blood Cold

Blood Stain

Blood Shot

Blood

You like it, I love it

You like it, I love it

You don't listen but react

You like it, I love it

You treat them better than me

You like it, I love it

You want me to be as miserable as you

You like it, I love it

You think your shit doesn't stink

You like it, I love it

You blame me for your problems

You like it, I love it

You can't stand my happiness

You like it, I love it

You think I'm better than you

You like it, I love it

If you like it, I will always love it

Frontin

Frontin

Emotions and Feelings

Frontin

Love and Hate

Frontin

Insecurities and Security

Frontin

Family and Friends

Frontin

Life and Death

Frontin

Poor and Rich

Frontin

Apology

Apology

Apology that doesn't come

Apology

Sincere Apology

Apology

Fake Apology

Apology

Sympathetic Apology

Apology

Understanding Apology

Apology

Misunderstood Apology

Apology

Apology that doesn't mean shit

Apology

Hurtful Apology

Apology

Painful Apology

Apology

Meaningful Apology

Apology

MY

My breath is taken away

My words don't mean a thing

Communication and understanding are thrown away

My actions are never enough

My love is taken for granted

Hearts are torn and bleed dry

My my my everything is never enough

Money

Green

Power

It's my money

Why you worry how I spend it

Why does it matter how much I got

You mad

You want to spend it up

It's my money

Greed

Green

My money not yours

Stop trying to count my coins

It's my money

Outsider

Outside the lines

Outside the box

Outside of the house

Outside of everything

Outside the norm

Different from others

Different languages

Stranger to the people you know

Different Period

Outsider

To LIVE

What does it mean to live?

Does it mean to take care of family?

Does it mean to take of children?

Does it mean to take vacations and party?

What does it mean to live?

Is it to take leap and bounds and risk?

Is it to explore and get to you yourself?

Is it to have that fling or romance or one night stand?

Is it to do the unthinkable?

What does it mean to live?

Is all those things above and more?

You have to live your life even with the mistakes and regrets and happy times

You have to live for you and fuck everything else

You may say I lived

Others will questioned how you lived

But NO matter what at least you lived

So enjoy the mistakes and regrets

Cuz you made changes and grew

So enjoy the happy times

Cuz at least you found what made you happy

You lived in the end

Black 1

Dark

Dreary

Scary

Imitated

Nothingness

Nobody

Nothing Special

Slave

Untrustworthy

Time

Gets Better over time

Gets Prettier over time

Gets Worse over time

Gets Uglier over time

Only Time knows how it will be

Only Time knows how that person is

Only Time knows the details

Only Time will tell you

Black 2

Strong

Resilient

Beautiful

Powerful

Admired

Kings & Queens

Envied

Intelligent

Copied/Followed

Influencers

Style

Flair

Hustlers

Swag

Children

Funny

Bothersome

Independent

Thinkers

Creative

Nosey

Noisy

Dreamers

Hormones

Motivation

Pains

Annoying

Precious

Lovable

Sneaky

Quiet

Talkers

Will tell your business

Greatest Gifts In The World

Light within you

Shine

Bright

Enlighten

Glow

Luminous

Gleaming

Everlasting

The Way I Speak

Words

Letters

Numbers

Characters

Keys

Chatter

Tones

Pitch

Deep

Low

Sounds

Accent

Clarity

Clear

Concise

Vulgar

Educated

Knowledgeable

Witt

Sass

Aggressive

Why can't you fuck me right

Why can't you fuck, sex and make love to me right

Damn I told you that I cum like the ocean

Damn you don't give me foreplay to make sure my vagina is most

Don't you understand I need that lubrication

Why can't you fuck, sex and me love to me right

You want me to suck your dick because you need head

Shit I need head too

I really don't want to give you head because I don't give head like that

I don't know where your dick been

You don't have to give me head

But why don't you fuck, sex and make love to me right

Listen stop telling me that I need to flip and reverse it

You need to stop listening to these rap songs

Because you damn sure ain't hitting it right

You need to take your ass to a sex class

You keep telling me what I'm doing wrong

But did you notice that my body isn't feelin you and your dick

Motherfucker I guess not because as long as you get your dick wet

Stop wasting my time

WHY CAN'T YOU FUCK, SEX OR MAKE LOVE TO ME RIGHT

DAMN DAMN DAMN!!!!

EXES

Why you think I miss you

I don't

Why you think I miss the dick

Boy, please you wasn't all that

Why you think I'm jealous because you have a new girl

Shit, I'm free of your drama

Why you all in my face

I don't want you

Why you still trying to call me

Blocked

But, let me leave a message first to tell you that your dick wasn't all that

I was your upgrade and not the other way around

I will still make money and you don't stop my shine over here

Is fucking all you think about

I'm not a piece of meat

I have feelings

Pounding and taking what you want

My body craves more

Do you know how to make me squirm quiver and shake?

Can you tell when I'm not overflowing with cum?

Do you know how to make my body adjust to you?

Do you even care?

I forgot I'm just a fuck to you

If you going to fuck me then at least do it right

Equality

What is EQUALITY?

You don't treat me as you're equal

As a woman I'm supposed to bow down and be your doormat

You look at my beauty but not my brains

I'm not going to be your sex toy or your house slave

You keep trying to break me

You pass me over on job titles

You put me against the other women

They do your bidding for you but don't realize their your slave or no their worth

You put fear into other hardworking women

You make them sacred to fight you

You try to break me

I still keep my head up high and keep getting back up

You can't understand why I'm not totally broken by you

I will keep my head up, be happy and not lose my self-respect

I DESERVE EQUALITY

Depression

Sadness

Insecurities

Ups and Downs

Good Days

Bad Days

Hopeless

Stressed

Moods

Wondering will it be better

Wondering will it end

Wondering is it all in my head

Wondering does anyone understand

Should I seek help or not

Communication

Why don't you talk with me?

Who cares if I'm long winded or not

Why is communicating so hard

How will you know how I feel?

Why should I hold it in?

Talking to me means getting to know me

No communication means no interaction or dealing with me

Spit

Creams

Oils

Vaseline

Tubes

Bottles

Sprays

Moisture

Moisture

Slimy

Wet

Moist

Sticky

Once

Twice

Multiples

Path

Straight

Narrow

Wide

Split

Left

Right

Wrong

Bumpy

Twist

Turns

Curves

Mistakes

Fair

Dark

Light

Cloudy

Visible

Steady

Growth

Learning

Cougar

Prowling

Looking

Liking

Contemplating

Doing

Observing

Exploration

Exhilarating

Fun

Fancy

Shameless

Seductive

Tempting

Tasting

Motions

What

What

What the fuck

What

What do you want

What

What is it you need

What

What do I do for you

What

What can I say

What

What will you do

What

What time is it

What

What will you do next

What

What will this accomplish

What

What

What the fuck

About the Author

Fun loving and colorful person that sees the world in various ways. She has children that are adventures within themselves. She always learning and growing within herself and going on new journeys in life. Until next time, please enjoy life and the adventures it may bring.